Black-Tie Spy

George Glass

SCHOLASTIC INC.

For Jan, who always sees me
as half-full.
— G.G.

ISBN 978-0-545-47271-5

Copyright © 2013 by George Glass

All rights reserved. Published by Scholastic Inc.

12 11 10 9 8 7 6 5 4 3   15 16 17/0

Printed in the U.S.A.   40
First Scholastic printing, December 2012

CHAPTER ONE

Marcos took a deep breath and blew into the balloon. As it stretched out, he looked around the park. He knew that not everyone around him was who they appeared to be. Some of them were in disguise.

He was in disguise, too. He was dressed as a clown, wearing a baggy red-and-blue-striped suit, big red shoes, and a red wig that stuck out around his head like a cloud. His face was painted white, and a huge smile was drawn on with red makeup. He even had a red foam ball attached to the tip of his nose. He was sure that nobody was going to see through his disguise.

I'm getting an A on this exam, he thought. *Maybe even an A plus*.

He was proud of himself. Disguise was a difficult class, and his teacher, M. Masque, was tough. All the teachers at SPY Academy were tough, but M. Masque's class was the one that gave Marcos the most trouble. He really wanted to do well on his midterm exam to prove that he was a good spy.

More than that, he wanted to beat Jen Bogart. Jen was one of his best friends, and she was good at *everything*. She never had trouble with her assignments, was always the first to raise her hand to answer a question posed by a teacher, and was at the top of almost every one of her classes. But she never bragged about it, so it was easy to like her. She and Marcos had become friends when they were paired together in Ippon Sensei's Martial Arts class. On her very first try, Jen had flipped Marcos over and onto his back. They'd been friends ever since.

The receiver in Marcos's ear buzzed. Then he heard M. Masque's voice.

"Jen has caught Narhari," his teacher said.

"That leaves only two players—Jen and Marcos. May the best spy win."

Marcos tied a knot in the end of the balloon and twisted it in the middle. A couple more twists, and the balloon turned into a horse. Marcos, scanning the park for signs of Jen, waved the balloon horse at a little girl who was standing nearby, watching him. She ran over and took it from him, smiling happily.

"Who else wants a balloon animal?" Marcos called out, changing his voice so that it was higher than usual. "I can make you an elephant, a dog, even a giraffe!"

Again he looked at the people moving around him as he inflated another balloon. They all looked perfectly ordinary. But one of them had to be Jen. *What would she disguise herself as?* he wondered.

Then he saw the mailman. Dressed in blue, he had a sack of letters slung over his shoulder. He had a large nose, bushy eyebrows, and a droopy mustache. He was walking quickly and looking from side to side.

That's Jen, Marcos thought. It was a great

disguise, but he saw right through it. That was Jen, all right.

His heart racing, he walked up to the mailman as quickly as he could. His big shoes made him waddle like a duck, and the balloon in his hand looked like a big, yellow sausage. He tapped the mailman on the shoulder with it.

"Got you!" Marcos said.

The mailman turned around and looked at him with a puzzled expression. "Excuse me?" he said.

Marcos laughed. "Good try, Jen," he said. "But no one has eyebrows that big, and that mustache is ridiculous."

The mailman's face turned red. "I don't know what kind of clown you are," he said angrily. "But you're certainly not the funny kind."

"I'm the kind of clown who does this," Marcos said, reaching out and giving the mailman's nose a squeeze. "Honk! Honk!" he said, laughing.

"How dare you!" the mailman yelled, holding his nose. "Why, I should report you to the police. I've never met such a rude clown!"

Suddenly, Marcos didn't feel so funny. Looking

at the mailman's furious expression, he wondered whether maybe he'd made a mistake. *But those eyebrows,* he thought. *They look like giant caterpillars. They can't be real.*

The mailman gave Marcos one last glare, then turned and stomped away, muttering something that sounded like "crazy clown." Marcos watched him go. It wasn't Jen in disguise, after all.

But that was okay, he told himself. He still had a chance to find her. All he had to do was focus. He took a deep breath and looked around him once more. Jen had to be somewhere.

"Excuse me."

An old lady was smiling at him. Her gray hair was tucked neatly under a hat covered in pink roses, and her thick glasses made her eyes look much bigger than they really were. Standing beside her was a little boy about six or seven years old. He stared at Marcos.

"Do you think you could make a balloon animal for my grandson?" the old woman asked.

Marcos nodded. "Sure," he said. "What would you like?"

The old lady looked at the little boy. "William, what animal would you like the nice clown to make for you?"

"An octopus," William said. "A purple one."

"One purple octopus," the woman told Marcos. "Please."

Marcos searched in his pockets for purple balloons. He pulled out a handful and blew up four of them, twisting them together until he had something with eight arms and a head. He handed it to William.

"There you go," he said. "One purple octopus."

William stared at the balloon animal. "It's not very good," he said, wrinkling his nose. "It looks like a spider, not an octopus."

"William!" his grandmother exclaimed. "You apologize to the nice clown right this minute."

"It's okay," Marcos said. He was anxious to get back to searching for Jen, and the woman and her grandson were taking up a lot of time.

"You apologize, young man," said the woman sternly.

William sighed. "I'm sorry, Marcos," he said.

"Really, it's—" Marcos stopped and looked at

the boy. "How do you know my name?" he asked.

William nodded at his grandmother. "She told me," he said. Then he turned to the old woman. "Can I have my dollar now?"

The woman opened her purse and pulled out a dollar. She handed it to William, who put it in his pocket and then turned and ran over to a woman who was sitting on a park bench.

"I'm afraid I'm not really his grandmother," the old woman said, her voice suddenly sounding much younger than it had earlier.

She reached up and took her hat off. Her gray hair came with it, revealing a head of brown hair underneath. As soon as he saw it, Marcos groaned.

"Got you!" Jen said.

"That's not fair, using a little kid," Marcos said, pretending to be mad. Well, he was mostly pretending. He really had wanted to win.

Jen laughed. "Good idea, wasn't it?" she said. "And he only cost me a buck."

"All right, you two. Bring it in." M. Masque's voice came through their receivers.

Marcos and Jen walked a block to where their teacher and the rest of their class were waiting beside the van in which they'd ridden into town that morning. As they got closer, the class applauded and Jen bowed.

"Congratulations," said M. Masque. "A fine job, both of you," he added, nodding at Marcos.

Marcos nodded back, thrilled at the compliment. Their teacher was a master of disguise, turning up as someone—or something—different every day. Today he was a pirate with a beard, a big hat, and even a real parrot on his shoulder. Marcos wondered what he looked like under the layers of makeup. As far as he knew, no one had ever seen M. Masque's real face.

"Fine job," the parrot squawked.

"All right, everybody," the teacher said. "Into the van."

Marcos, Jen, and the others piled into the van. As they drove back to the St. Perfidious Yearling Academy for Excellence, Marcos thought ahead to his next midterm exam. It was in Strategy, a class he loved. But he was a little anxious about the test. The teacher, Professor Booker, hadn't given them any clue about what to expect. Marcos had been worrying about it all week.

"What's the matter?" Jen asked, elbowing him in the side. "The other clowns steal your flower that squirts water?"

Marcos laughed. "Keep it up, old lady," he said. "You haven't seen my pie-in-the-face trick yet."

"You wouldn't pie an old granny, would you?" said Jen in a creaky voice.

"Try me," Marcos said as the van pulled up to the main entrance to the school.

Jen opened the van door and got out. "See you in Strategy in half an hour," she said. "I hope you're ready."

Marcos pointed a finger at her. "Bring it on," he said.

CHAPTER TWO

Good afternoon," Professor Cornelius Booker said as he walked into the classroom and shut the door behind him.

The conversations that had been going on stopped as the five students seated at the single long table in the room sat at attention. Professor Booker wasn't just their Strategy professor; he was also the principal of SPY Academy, and everyone wanted to make a good impression whenever he was around.

"I understand Miss Bogart is to be congratulated on her performance in this morning's Disguise examination," the teacher said.

He nodded at Jen, who nodded back. Although she acted as though being complimented by Principal Booker was no big deal, Marcos could tell she was fighting hard not to smile. He kicked her foot lightly under the table, trying to make her laugh, but she just kicked him back and looked straight ahead.

"Mr. Elias," Principal Booker said sharply.

Marcos straightened up. "Yes, sir!" he said. He held his breath, waiting for the teacher to reprimand him for fooling around.

"You seem to have missed a spot of greasepaint on your left ear."

Marcos put his hand to his ear and rubbed. His fingers came away covered in white clown makeup.

The other students laughed as Principal Booker walked over and handed Marcos a tissue. Marcos, blushing with embarrassment, took it and wiped away the remaining makeup.

"By the way," Principal Booker said as he walked back to his desk, "the word on the street is that you make a very fine balloon giraffe."

Again everyone laughed, including Marcos. "I try, sir," he said.

"Perhaps one day you'll show me how it's done," the principal said. "Whenever I attempt it I always manage to wind up with an extra leg."

Marcos waited for Principal Booker to start handing out the tests. Instead, he put his hands in his pockets, seemed to think for a moment, then asked, "Can any of you tell me who Napoleon Coin was?"

Marcos glanced over at Jen, who for once didn't have her hand raised. Marcos didn't recognize the name, either.

"Napoleon Coin was the head of North Star Communications," said Sheila Bell.

Marcos looked down the table at Sheila, whom everyone called Tinker, or Tink, because of her proficiency with gadgets of all kinds. She was the best pupil in Dr. O's Tech class, making it the one class Jen Bogart wasn't the star of. Tinker didn't talk much, and sometimes it seemed that she was more interested in machines than in people, but she could be really funny when you got to know her. She also had really cool dreadlocks and always seemed to know about the newest video games before anyone else did. She was what Agent 4, the Stealth teacher, called an enigma.

"That's right," Principal Booker said. "Very good, Miss Bell. And what else do you know about him?"

"He got his start in newspapers," Tinker said. "Then he got into radio and television. Now he owns the largest network of communication satellites in the world. Well, owned. He died a few years ago."

"Very good," said the teacher. "Anything else?"

Everyone looked at Tinker, who kept going. "He was an inventor. He created a lot of the spy technology we use today. That's about all I know."

"You know more than most people," Principal Booker said, raising one eyebrow and looking at the other four students as if they, too, should have known these things. "What you don't know is that Napoleon Coin was a very dear friend of mine. We worked together on a number of occasions, and I was fortunate enough to have gone on several adventures with him."

"Adventures?" Marcos said, suddenly more

interested than he had been a moment before.

"Yes, Mr. Elias, adventures," said Principal Booker. "Napoleon Coin was one of the last great explorers. He liked nothing more than a mystery, and would often drop everything to set off into the jungle, or under the sea, or anywhere else he thought he might find something interesting."

"What kinds of things?" asked Zeke Slick, who was sitting on Marcos's right. Redheaded, athletic, and outgoing, Zeke was the class jock. He could sometimes be loud, and he was a little too fond of punching you in the shoulder when he liked you, but he was a good guy. He was also Marcos's roommate at the academy.

"Mummies," the teacher said in answer to Zeke's question. "Ruins of ancient civilizations. Jewels. One of his greatest finds was the Blue Carbuncle."

"What's a carbuncle?" Marcos asked.

"A gemstone," Principal Booker explained. "Usually a red one. But this one is blue. In fact, it's the only blue one ever found. It's also the largest."

"What makes it blue?" asked Narhari Dhawan.

"That's the most interesting part," their teacher

said. "The Blue Carbuncle contains an element found nowhere else in the world. That we know of, anyway. It's called napolium, after Napoleon, of course. It's what makes the Blue Carbuncle so valuable."

"What's a stone like that worth?" Zeke asked.

Principal Booker gave a little smile. "It's priceless," he said.

Marcos, who had wanted to ask the question for a while now, finally said, "Excuse me, but what does Napoleon Coin have to do with our midterm?"

Principal Booker cocked a finger at Marcos. "An excellent question," he said. "And I was just about to get to that."

The five students waited expectantly while Principal Booker looked at them. He seemed to be thinking about something, as if he was trying to make up his mind. Finally, he nodded and said, "Yes, I think you're ready."

Ready for what? Marcos wondered. The exam? He didn't know whether he was ready, but he wanted to get started on it and get it over with. He wished the teacher would just get on with it.

"Normally at this point in the semester I would give you a hypothetical case and ask you to plan a strategy for handling it," the principal said. "But you're one of the best classes I've ever had—don't let that go to your heads—and I think for you I'm going to do something different. Something more difficult," he added.

Several of the students groaned.

"What?" said Principal Booker. "You aren't ready for something difficult? Should I just hand out the ordinary test I usually give?"

He held up a stack of papers. "I have it right here."

"No," Jen said. She looked at the other four students. "We're ready. Right, guys?"

"Right," they all said.

Principal Booker set the tests down. "Good," he said. "Then instead of the hypothetical case, I'm giving you a real one. You're going to keep the Blue Carbuncle from being stolen."

"Really?" Marcos said.

"Really," said the teacher.

"Who's going to steal it?" Narhari asked.

"My brother is," Principal Booker answered. "Well, one of his students is. He never does the difficult work himself. At least, that's what I believe he's going to try to do."

Principal Cornelius Booker's brother, Maximus, was as bad as Cornelius was good. He ran a school called the ROGUE School, which stood for Receivers of a Genuinely Unsavory Education. His students went on to be the bad guys that SPY Academy graduates often fought against. The brothers were fierce rivals, and any crime that involved them trying to outdo each other was sure to be dangerous—and exciting.

"My intelligence suggests that Maximus wants to steal the Blue Carbuncle and use it for his own dastardly purposes."

"What purposes?" Jen asked.

"That's the thing," said Principal Booker. "I don't know. All my informant knows, and consequently all I know, is that he wants it. But I don't think he wants to sell it. You see, the Carbuncle is more than just a gem. It's a key."

"A key to what?" said Marcos.

"An invention," the teacher said. "According to Napoleon, the greatest invention the world has ever seen."

"I bet it's a satellite," Tinker said, sounding more excited than Marcos had ever heard her. "I bet it combines all the different kinds of communication technology into one super-satellite."

"Maybe," said Principal Booker. "Maybe not. Napoleon never told me what it is. I don't think he told anyone what it is. All he said was that it was going to change the world."

"But why now?" Zeke asked. "You said Napoleon Coin died a few years ago. If Maximus wanted the Carbuncle, why has he waited all this time to try and steal it?"

Professor Booker smiled. "Because until now it's been locked away in a safe to which only one person in the world has the combination. And that person is me. I have never written the combination down. It's kept in here." He tapped on his forehead with one finger.

"Why are you taking it out of the safe?" Marcos asked him.

Principal Booker sighed. "Because later this

week Napoleon's grandson, Titus, is turning twelve," he said. "And on his twelfth birthday he receives his inheritance, an inheritance that includes the Blue Carbuncle. He will then be the richest young man on the planet."

Marcos couldn't help but notice that the principal didn't sound very happy about this. "Isn't that a lot for one kid to have?" he said.

"Indeed it is," said the teacher. "And it presents all kinds of dangers to Mr. Titus Coin. Which is where you all come in. On Saturday night there is to be a birthday party for Titus. Only young people are invited. And not just any young people. The guests will be the richest, most famous young people from all over the world. There will be no adults present. And during this party the Blue Carbuncle will be revealed for the first time since going into storage."

"You think the ROGUE kids are going to infiltrate the party and try to steal it," Jen said.

"That's right," said Principal Booker. "And the five of you will be there to make sure that doesn't happen."

He picked up five thick folders and handed

one to each of them. "These dossiers will tell you everything you need to know about Titus and his guests. It will be up to you to work together to formulate a plan for protecting Titus and the Carbuncle, identifying the ROGUE spies, and, if possible, finding out the nature of the invention for which the Carbuncle is an integral part."

"So, if the Carbuncle is stolen, we fail?" said Zeke.

"But it won't be stolen," Jen said. As always, she was the one who tried to unite them as a team. "So we won't fail. Right?" She looked at the others.

"Right," they all answered.

CHAPTER THREE

That evening after dinner, the five members of Principal Booker's Strategy class met in the library to plan. They sat around a table in the back, where they could talk without bothering anyone. Each of them had a dossier filled with intelligence that had been gathered about Titus Coin, the Blue Carbuncle, and the upcoming party.

"Let's take a look at the guest list first," Marcos suggested, removing a sheet of paper from his folder.

They took a minute to scan the list of names.

"Wow," said Zeke. "It looks like everybody is coming to this thing."

"Everybody who's rich," remarked Tinker. "I mean, Fanta and Shasta Popp? Come on. What have they ever done except have money and go to parties? Their dad is the one who's the king of sodas. They're just princesses."

"Not everyone on here is like that," Narhari said. "Basil Twilly is a crossword puzzle champion, and Kat Barlowe won the International Science Prize last year for inventing an engine that runs on air."

"How do you know all this?" Zeke asked her.

"For one thing, it's all written down here," said Narhari, rolling her eyes. "For another, I'm into this stuff. We don't all spend our time working out," she added, teasing Zeke.

"JJ Jay," Marcus read, continuing down the list. "Isn't he a singer?"

Jen groaned. "He's so annoying," she said. Then, imitating a boy's voice, she sang, "'Baby, baby, baby. Oh, baby, you're my baby.'"

"He sings that?" said Marcos. "I kind of like that song." He hummed the popular tune while continuing to look over the guest list. Jen glared at him, and he pretended to ignore her, humming more loudly.

"Anya is going to be there," Tinker said.

"Anya who?" asked Narhari.

"Just Anya," Tinker told her. "The Russian model."

"Since when are you up on famous models?" Narhari said.

Tinker shrugged. "A girl can't read technical manuals *all* the time," she said.

"Is there anybody normal on this list?" said Zeke. "You know, anyone who's just a kid?"

"Some of them are the kids of political leaders," Jen said. "Not that having a mother for a prime minister is exactly normal, but it's more normal than being a teenage Russian model or the world's biggest pop star."

"So how are we going to blend in with all these people?" asked Narhari. "We're going to stick out if we don't come up with some good disguises."

"We don't all have to be disguised," Marcos said, thinking hard. "A lot of this will be behind-the-scenes stuff. You know, communications and keeping an eye on Titus and all of that. Only a couple of us need to actually be out there with the other guests."

"Marcos is right," said Tinker. "If we each concentrate on what we're good at, some of us won't even be seen. Like I'll take care of all the technical stuff, and I can do that from anyplace in the mansion."

"And Zeke is great at surveillance," said Jen. "So why don't you be in charge of tracking the movements of all the guests?"

"Good idea," Zeke agreed. "We can use those cool new cameras Tink designed."

"I guess that means I'll be guarding Titus, then," said Narhari, the martial arts expert.

"Only he can't know you're guarding him," Jen reminded her. "No one knows about us, even him. So you'll need some kind of alias."

"What about you?" Marcos asked Jen. "I assume that as the master of disguise, you'll be dressed up like a plant or something. I know—a giant cake!"

"Ha-ha," said Jen. "Actually, I think I'm going to be a server. It says in here that the party is being catered, and all of the servers will be kids. I'll dress as one of them and carry trays around. That will give me a chance to watch everybody up close."

"That leaves Marcos," said Zeke.

They all looked at him.

"What?" Marcos said.

"You *know* what," Jen said. "Out of all of us, you're the best schmoozer."

"Yeah," agreed Narhari. "You can talk to anybody."

"And get them to tell you anything," Tinker added. "You got me to tell you about your own surprise birthday party last year, remember? I didn't even realize I was saying anything until I'd already said it."

Marcos grinned. "That was pretty sweet," he said.

"Then it's settled," said Jen. "Marcos will use his charm on the guests to see what kind of information he can get out of them."

"He'll need an alias," Zeke said. "He can't just be Marcos."

"True," said Jen. "So, who do you want to be?" she asked Marcos.

"I can be a video-game designer. I'll say I work for one of the big gaming companies coming up with ideas. Nobody can question that as long as I don't claim I've worked on any familiar games."

"Good thinking," said Narhari. "And you can still use your real name, which means you won't forget who you're supposed to be. Again."

"That was just *one* time," Marcos objected. "And you try being named Rufus Xavier Sarsaparilla. It's not easy."

"Then we all know our jobs," Jen said. "Tinker will keep us linked up, Narhari will shadow Titus, Zeke will monitor the situation, Marcos will gather intel, and I'll—"

"Be serving shrimp puffs," said Marcos.

Everyone laughed, including Jen. For a moment Marcos forgot that they weren't talking about a pretend scenario. But then he remembered—this was the real thing. Not only did their grade in the class depend on their performance, so did Titus Coin's safety and the safety of the Blue Carbuncle.

"Are you guys nervous?" Tinker asked.

No one spoke for a long moment. Then Zeke said, "Maybe a little."

"Me, too," said Jen. "But just a *really* little.

About this much." She held two fingertips very close together, so that there was just a sliver of space between them.

"It's good that we're nervous," Marcos said.

"A *little* nervous," Narhari reminded him.

"A little nervous," said Marcos. "It will keep us focused on what we have to do. We can do this if we work as a team."

He held out his hand with the palm facing the floor. "I declare Operation Carbuncle officially begun!" he said. "Who's with me?"

One by one the others put their hands in, until five hands formed a stack.

Marcos counted out, "One! Two! Three!"

"Go team!" they all shouted.

"*Shh!*" someone hissed.

They turned to see the librarian, Mr. Perkins, glaring at them over his glasses, his finger pressed to his lips.

"Sorry," Marcos said. He looked at the others. "Go team!" he whispered, as they all started to laugh.

CHAPTER FOUR

The Coin mansion was unlike anything Marcos had ever seen. Well, anything outside of a movie. It was absolutely huge, covering the entire top of a hill overlooking the town. A winding drive-way led to a set of wrought-iron gates that were guarded by two big men wearing black suits and sunglasses.

Marcos and Narhari sat in the back of the limo. Marcos was wearing a tuxedo, and Narhari was wearing a pretty red dress and a diamond neck-lace. Her long, black hair, which she usually kept in a neat braid, was loose and fell past her shoul-ders. Neither of them had ever worn such fancy clothes, and Marcos kept pulling at the bow tie around his neck.

The next time he reached for the tie, Narhari slapped his hand away. "Stop it," she said. "You can't do that during the party."

Marcos groaned. "I don't know how people wear these," he said. "I feel like I'm choking."

"How do you think I feel?" said Narhari. "Look at this dress. How am I supposed to do karate in this thing?"

The driver stopped at the gate and the guards checked the invitations Principal Booker had provided, scanning them with handheld devices before nodding to the limo driver and opening the gates with a remote control. As the car slipped through, Marcos wondered how Jen, Zeke, and Tinker were doing. They had arrived at the mansion a few hours before, so that they could get set up before the party began.

"Look at this place," Narhari said as the limo came to a stop in the circular driveway that passed in front of the house. "It's not a house; it's a castle."

The driver got out, opened the back door, and helped Narhari out. Marcos followed, and the two of them walked up the steps to the front doors of the mansion, which were flanked by two more guards.

Their tickets were checked one final time, and then they were inside. They had seen blueprints of the house as part of their dossiers, but the real thing was like nothing they had ever seen. Huge paintings of serious-looking people, beautiful landscapes, and ships on the ocean hung on the walls. Chandeliers dripping in crystals hung over their heads. There was even a statue of a woman holding a bowl of fruit that looked so real Marcos was tempted to try to take a banana out of it.

A butler greeted them and led them down a wood-paneled hallway to another set of doors. Marcos had never seen a real live butler before, and wondered whether he was supposed to offer him a tip. But the man just opened the doors and bowed his head slightly before turning and walking away.

Marcos and Narhari found themselves in a room filled with people. Kids were everywhere, drinking from fancy glasses and taking food from the trays being carried around by waiters and waitresses. Marcos saw Jen carrying a tray of little cakes. She came over to him and Narhari and held the tray out.

"Would you like a lemon cake?" she asked, as if she had never seen them before in her life.

"Thank you," Narhari said, taking one.

"Thanks," said Marcos as he took one as well.

As he took it, Jen leaned in and said, "So far we haven't seen anything suspicious. But Titus is about to make his appearance, so be on the lookout."

She turned and walked away, offering the tray to a pair of pretty girls who stood nearby. They were wearing identical pink dresses, and Marcos realized they were twins.

"The Popp twins," Narhari said. "Shasta and Fanta. And over there is Basil Twilly."

Marcos looked over and saw a short, slightly fat young man dressed in a wool suit complete with a vest. He looked out of place surrounded by all the well-dressed guests, but he didn't seem to care. He was talking loudly to another boy, whom Marcos recognized instantly.

"That's JJ Jay," he whispered. "He's shorter than he looks in his videos."

JJ Jay was wearing a white tuxedo and a white cap covered in what looked like diamonds. This was his trademark, along with the thick gold necklace he wore that had three Js on it, also covered in diamonds. JJ had a confused look on his face as he listened to Basil talk.

"He can't understand Basil because of his accent," Narhari said.

Marcos recalled then that Basil was English. He was the crossword puzzle champion, and Marcos wondered what he could be talking about with America's biggest pop star.

There was a slight buzzing in his ear. Then Tinker's voice came through. She had given them each a tiny earpiece to wear. The device could also pick up anything they said, so they were able to communicate with one another easily, as long as they didn't all talk at once.

"Tinker here," said Tinker. "Marcos and Narhari, are you there?"

"I'm here," Narhari said.

"Here," said Marcos.

"Jen?" Tinker said. "Can you hear us?"

"Would you like a lemon cake?" said Jen.

Tinker laughed. "She can hear us," she said. "Zeke?"

There was silence as they waited for Zeke to check in. Finally he said, "What?"

Tinker sighed. "Can you hear us?" she asked.

"Yeah," Zeke answered. "Sorry. I was checking out the rooms on the second floor, and I got stuck in a closet."

"What were you doing in the closet?" Tinker said. Then she said, "Never mind. You're out now, right?"

"Right," Zeke confirmed. "I'm making my way back to the ballroom."

"Good," said Tinker. "Everyone keep those devices in your ears. If you lose them, you'll be out of contact and we can't help you. Tinker out."

The earpiece went silent. Just then, a door at one end of the room opened and a boy entered. Tall, thin, and blond, he had a narrow face and hair that was slicked back. He stopped every few feet to shake hands with guests and say hello, and he seemed very friendly. He was, of course, Titus Coin.

Titus made his way to a raised platform in the middle of the room. Marcos guessed that this was where the musicians sat when the room was used as a ballroom. Now it was empty except for a stone pedestal about five feet tall. Something sat on top of the pedestal, covered by a blue velvet cloth.

"Welcome, everyone!" Titus said cheerfully and loudly. "Thank you for coming to my birthday party!"

The room erupted in applause. When it died down, Titus continued.

"I'm really excited about tonight," he said. "First of all, I want you to know that there are only kids here tonight. All the adults have been sent away now that you're here, so there's no one to tell us to go to bed, to not eat as much cake and ice cream as we want to, or anything else. Tonight it's all about what *we* want to do."

The applause was even louder for this announcement, and there were even some whistles and shouts of "All right!" and "Yeah!"

"In a moment I'll announce a fun game we're going to play tonight," Titus told the group. "But first, I want to show you something."

He pointed to the pedestal and snapped his fingers. As if by magic, the cloth covering the top was lifted into the air and disappeared somewhere in the ceiling, revealing a glass case in which sat a huge blue stone.

There were gasps all around as people realized they were looking at the Blue Carbuncle. About the size of an orange, it sparkled under the lights in the case, glowing a light blue color.

"It's so beautiful," Narhari said.

"It's okay," said a voice next to Marcos. He looked over and saw one of the Popp twins standing beside him. "I've seen prettier stones."

"The Great Eye of Kali is bigger," said her sister, who was standing beside Narhari. "That's a ruby owned by Parni Chittor," she told Marcos, as if he should know who that was.

"Famous Bollywood actress," Narhari told him. "My brother Manoj has a *huge* crush on her."

"My grandfather discovered the Blue Carbuncle while searching for the lost city of Atlantis," Titus continued. "It was buried in the ruins." He paused.

"I wish he was here tonight to celebrate my birthday," he said.

Marcos felt bad for Titus. He obviously missed his grandfather. Marcos thought about his own grandfather, who was still alive, and promised himself he would visit him during the next school break.

"But I know he would want us to have fun tonight," said Titus, sounding happier. "So in his honor, we're going to have a treasure hunt."

A murmur of excitement went through the crowd. Titus grinned. "I thought you might like that," he said.

All of a sudden, doors around the room opened and servers carrying silver trays entered. On the trays were envelopes.

"You've been put into groups of seven participants," Titus explained as the servers passed among the crowd, handing out the envelopes. "Each team will be searching for a different treasure. The first team to find their item and return here wins a prize. Now, please find the others in your group and get started on your first clue."

CHAPTER FIVE

A waiter handed Marcos and Narhari their envelopes. Marcos opened his and looked at the list of his team members.

"We're on different teams," Narhari said. "I guess I'll see you later. Be careful, and keep your eyes open."

"Who is Marcos Elias?" said one of the Popp twins.

"I am," Marcos told her.

The girl looked at Marcos with a puzzled expression on her face. "But who *are* you?" she asked. "I've never heard of you."

"It seems we've been thrown together for this little escapade," said a voice with a British accent before Marcos could try out his alias on the Popp girl.

Basil Twilly waved his paper at them, and the Popp twins exchanged disappointed glances. But they brightened up when JJ Jay came up to the group and said, "Hey there, teammates. What's up?"

The Popp twins giggled.

"That leaves Kat Barlowe," Marcos said, looking at the list.

"Did someone say my name?" A girl joined them. Small and serious looking, she had short, dark hair and intense eyes. She was wearing a dress that didn't fit very well and was a little out of style, and she looked really uncomfortable in it. She glanced at the Popp twins and added, "This should be fun," in a tone that sounded like she thought it would be anything but.

"That makes six," Basil said. "We're missing someone."

"That would be me," said a strong voice. It also was accented, but unlike Basil's British one, it was more foreign sounding.

"Anya," said JJ. "Good to see you again."

The Russian model looked at JJ and smiled. "I'm sure it is," she said.

"They went out for a while," Marcos heard Tinker say in his earpiece. "She broke up with him. His song 'Heartbreaker' is about her."

"Then that's it," said a Popp twin.

"Not quite." Unexpectedly, Titus Coin came up and joined the group. "I'm your last member."

"But your name isn't on the list," said Basil.

"And that makes . . ." One of the Popp girls counted on her fingers. She looked confused, then started over.

"Eight," Kat said impatiently.

"That's one too many," said the Popp girl, frowning.

"I believe Chrysanthemum is counting you and your sister as one person," Titus told her.

"I hate it when people do that," said the other twin.

"Right?" said the first one. "I mean, we're so different."

Marcos, who still couldn't tell Shasta from Fanta, looked at Kat, who shook her head and sighed.

"Anyway," Titus said, ignoring them, "here I am. As for my name not being on the list, Chrysanthemum said she wanted it to be a surprise."

"Who's Chrysanthemum?" asked JJ.

"Chrysanthemum Budge," Titus explained. "My grandfather's secretary. She was with him for more than thirty years. Now she organizes everything to do with his foundation."

"Well, then," Anya said. "Now that we all know one another, what's our first clue?"

"That will be on the back of the list," Titus answered.

Marcos flipped his paper over. "'Go down the hole and through the glass into the land of wonder. Look for the dumb twins and they'll tell you where to go next.'"

"'The dumb twins'?" said Kat. "I think we've already found them."

"Where?" asked one of the Popps, looking around.

Basil Twilly was peering at the clue, squinting his eyes. The tip of his tongue stuck out between his lips, and he seemed to be humming. After a minute he smiled broadly and said, "I know what it means."

"What is it?" JJ asked.

Basil turned to Titus. "Which way is the library?" he asked.

"Down the hall," said Titus, pointing to a door. "That way."

Basil turned and marched toward the door. After a few steps he turned again and looked over his shoulder at the others. "Well?" he said. "Are you coming or not?"

"Where are we going?" a Popp twin asked.

Basil sighed. "Isn't it obvious?" he said. "To Wonderland."

Marcos's earpiece clicked on as they walked down the hall. It was Zeke.

"Marcos, since Narhari is on another team and you've got Titus on yours, you're going to have to look out for him."

"Got it," Marcos said in a low voice.

"Try not to lose him," Zeke said, teasing.

"I'll try," said Marcos. "But no promises."

The Coin library was almost as big as the one at St. Perfidious. Heavy dark wood shelves stretched from floor to ceiling, each one filled with books. Ladders attached to rails on the shelves rolled on a track in the floor, so that you could move them around and climb up to even the highest shelves. Several big armchairs were placed around the room, each one with a light positioned beside it, making them great spots for sitting in and reading. There were even some nooks built into the shelves at various heights, each lined with cushions and featuring built-in lights, perfect for curling up with a favorite book.

"As you can see, my grandfather loved reading," Titus said. "He spent as much time in here as he did in his laboratory. He always said that there are as many adventures in books as there are in the real world."

Basil was busily looking at the shelves, running his fingers across the spines of the books and muttering to himself.

"They don't seem to be in any particular order," he said. "It's going to be difficult to find the book."

"What book is that?" Marcos asked.

Basil shot him a look. "I thought I already explained that," he said. "Down the hole? Through the glass? The clue is talking about Alice and her adventures in Wonderland. We need to find *Alice's Adventure in Wonderland.* But I have no idea where it might be."

"It should be over here," said Titus, walking to a ladder and beginning to climb up it. "This is where all the books about rabbits are."

"Rabbits?" Kat said. "Why would it be in books about rabbits? I mean, I know the White Rabbit is one of the characters, but he's not even the main one."

Titus laughed. "My grandfather didn't exactly think like everybody else does," he said. "He used to read the Alice books to me, and he liked the White Rabbit the best. So did I. So he put the books in the section about rabbits, so I would always be able to find them."

"That makes absolutely no sense," Basil remarked. "Fiction should be arranged alphabetically by the author's name, or by title. Not by . . . rabbits."

Titus stopped at a shelf and looked at the books

there. He ignored Basil as he selected a book and climbed down again.

"Here we are," he said. *"Alice's Adventures in Wonderland."*

"Now what do we do with it?" asked one of the Popps. "We don't have to read it, do we?"

"Fortunately for you, I already have," Basil told her. "Several times. That's how I know what the second part of the clue means."

"The dumb twins," Kat reminded them a little loudly, earning her a scowl from the Popps.

"Right," said Basil as he turned the pages of the book. "Ah, and here they are."

He held the book out so that everyone could see. It was open to a picture of two odd-looking characters standing side by side, each with an arm around the other's shoulders. They were dressed exactly alike, right down to the hats on their heads. The only difference between them was that one had the word *DEE* written on his shirt collar and the other had *DUM* on his.

"Tweedledee and Tweedledum," Marcos said. "The dumb twins."

The Popp girls sniffed. "They could be the Dee twins, too," one of them said.

"It's a play on words," said Basil. "Tweedle*dum* is one of the twins, but they're both *dumb*. Get it?"

"No," said the Popps. "Why are they dumb?"

"You'll have to read the book," Basil said. "Trust me, they're dumb."

"But where's the next clue?" Marcos asked. "They're supposed to tell us where to go next."

"Maybe it's written on one of the pages," Kat suggested.

Basil fanned the pages of the book, and a piece of paper fluttered to the ground. Marcos bent and picked it up. When he unfolded it he saw a diagram of the Coin mansion. Along one side of the map was a row of letters in alphabetical order. Along the top was a row of numbers, also in order.

Titus took the paper and studied it. "That's the second floor," he said. "But what's this at the bottom?"

Underneath the picture was a series of letters and numbers. They obviously corresponded to the letters and numbers on the map, but Marcos couldn't figure out what the series was supposed to mean. By the looks on the faces of the others around him, they didn't know, either.

Then Anya stepped up. "Let me see that," she said.

Titus handed her the paper. She looked at it for a minute, then laughed. "Very clever," she said.

"What is?" asked Kat.

"This puzzle," Anya replied.

"Is it a secret code?" asked a Popp twin.

"It's a code," Anya answered. "But it's not secret, at least not to someone who plays chess. This is a famous chess problem."

"And how do you know about it?" said Kat.

Anya looked at her. "Just because I'm pretty, that doesn't mean I'm stupid. I happen to be a very good chess player. My father is a grand champion. I've played since I was old enough to hold a chess piece."

Marcos, impressed, asked, "So what does this say?"

Anya pointed to the paper. "Each room on the map is like a square on a chessboard," she explained. "This code at the bottom tells us where the pieces move." She looked at them. "We're the pieces."

"So we just follow the moves, then," said Titus.

Anya shook her head. "The only room that matters is the last one. The puzzle takes us up to the move before that one. To find the right room, we have to solve it. Do you have a chessboard?" she asked Titus.

"There's one over here," Titus said, pointing to another table. "My grandfather loved to play chess. He tried to teach me, but I never really understood it."

Anya went to the chessboard and positioned the pieces on it. Marcos watched her move them around as she checked the moves against the code on the map. Eventually there were only a few pieces on the board.

"And the knight takes the queen," Anya said. "Checkmate." She then looked at the map and pointed to a room. "What is this room?"

Titus looked. "That's the music room," he said.

Anya nodded. "That's where we go next."

CHAPTER SIX

As they were walking up the stairs to the music room, Marcos heard his earpiece come on.

"Marcos, it's Tinker. We've got a problem. Someone has been trying to jam the transmitter to your earpiece for the last fifteen minutes. I don't even know if you can hear me. I hope you can. You need to be careful. They're onto us."

The earpiece crackled. Tinker said something else, but her voice was drowned out by a loud buzzing. Then there was silence.

"Tink?" Marcos whispered. "Tink? Are you there?"

There was no reply.

For a moment he panicked. But he remembered his training and calmed himself. He could handle the situation. All he had to do was remain cool. He thought back to what Principal Booker had taught them in Strategy class. The first thing to do was identify the main problem. That was easy. Someone—probably a ROGUE operative—had infiltrated the party. He or she might even be one of the members of his own group.

He studied the others. Could one of them be a ROGUE spy? It seemed unlikely that any of the famous people would be, but you never knew. After all, no one knew he was a spy, not even his own family, who thought he was attending a prestigious prep school. The students of SPY Academy studied in secret. When it came down to it, everyone at the party was a suspect. The only thing he could do was keep his eyes and ears open and be ready for action.

The music room was smaller than the library, but just as impressive. In the center of the room was a grand piano. All around it were different places to sit—couches and chairs—all covered in black velvet. The walls were painted a bright red and had a shiny look to them.

"Well?" said one of the Popps, looking at Anya.

"How should I know?" Anya said, shrugging. "I got us here. It's somebody else's turn to figure out why we're here." She sat down in one of the chairs and looked at her nails.

The others walked around the room, looking for clues. Marcos noticed that Kat was following Titus and talking to him. He quietly moved closer to them as he pretended to be looking underneath the cushions on a couch.

"I'm very interested in your grandfather's work," Kat told Titus.

"Uh-huh," said Titus, busily poking around inside a large vase that looked really old and really expensive.

"I consider him one of my heroes, actually," Kat continued. "I understand he was working on some very interesting projects when he died. You don't happen to know what those were about, do you?"

"Not really," Titus said, moving on. "He worked on all kinds of things."

"Yes, I know," Kat said. "But there must have been *one* thing he was most interested in."

Marcos wondered why Kat was so interested in what Napoleon Coin had been working on. She was a science genius herself, so maybe she was just curious. *Or maybe she's trying to find out what the Blue Carbuncle is the key to,* he thought.

Could Kat be the ROGUE spy? There was no reason why not. In fact, she was just the sort of person Maximus Booker might want on his team. She was smart and persistent, and Marcos could tell she didn't give up until she'd found the answers she was looking for.

"Maybe it had to do with lasers," Kat suggested. "Or particle acceleration. Just stop and think for a minute."

"I *am* thinking," Titus said, sounding annoyed. "I'm thinking about finding the next clue. And so should you."

He walked off, leaving Kat staring at his back. Marcos, sensing a chance to get more information, stepped over to her.

"He's kind of rude, isn't he?" he said.

Kat snorted. "Spoiled little rich kid," she said. "He has no idea how brilliant his grandfather was."

"Do you really think he was working on

something to do with lasers?" Marcos asked.

"I don't know." Kat shrugged. "I was just guessing. But I don't think Titus knows anything."

Marcos nodded, but in his mind he was wondering whether Kat was telling the truth or whether she was a skilled liar. On the one hand, if she knew he was a spy for the other side, she wouldn't want him to know anything. On the other hand, she might want him to *think* he knew what she was up to. Or she might not even know that *he* was a spy. It was hard to tell. He needed more information.

"I give up," Basil said, sitting down on a couch across from Anya. "Maybe we're in the wrong room," he added, looking at the model.

Anya's eyes narrowed. "We're in the right room," she said. "If you don't believe me, why don't you figure out the chess problem for yourself? Oh, that's right—you don't play chess."

Basil blushed and stammered something Marcos couldn't hear. Marcos could tell that a fight was likely to start if he didn't do something, so he cleared his throat and said, "Let's think about this. If the clue in the library had to do with books, then it makes sense that the clue in the music room would have something to do with music."

"Good thinking," said Kat. "But how would you hide a clue in music?"

Marcos thought hard. Then an idea came to him. "Maybe it's in a music book," he said. "There must be some in here somewhere."

"There's a whole bunch of sheet music over here," said JJ, who was standing in front of a cabinet that he'd opened. Inside were piles of music books.

Everybody except Anya went to look at the music.

"But how do we know where to start?" asked one of the Popp sisters. "There are millions of books in there."

"Did your grandfather have any favorite pieces of music?" Marcos asked.

Titus thought for a moment, as if he was waiting for someone else to answer the question. "He liked Grieg," he finally said.

"Greg?" said Kat. "Greg who?"

Titus frowned and rubbed his ear, again looking as if he hoped someone else would provide the answer. *"Grieg,"* he said. "Not Greg. He liked Grieg. Edvard Grieg."

"I've never heard of him," one Popp twin said to the other. "Have you?"

"Isn't he the guy Alexandra Rothstone brought to the Christmas ball last year?" she said.

"Edvard Grieg is a famous Norwegian composer," JJ said. "And he died in 1907, so I doubt Alexandra Rothstone brought him to the Christmas ball."

Marcos looked at JJ with interest. "You're into classical music?" he asked.

JJ looked away. "I just know a few things," he said. "That's all."

"Well, let's see if there's anything by Edvard Grieg in this cabinet," Kat said.

She began to leaf through the books as the others looked over her shoulder. Eventually she pulled one out. "Here we go," she said. "Grieg piano pieces."

"Shake it and see if a clue falls out," Titus told her.

Kat shook the book. No note fluttered out, so she shook it harder. When still nothing came out, she fanned the pages slowly.

"There's nothing here," she said, sounding disappointed.

"Maybe we're thinking about it the wrong way," said JJ.

Again Marcos looked at him with surprise. He'd barely said anything during the treasure hunt. Now he seemed to be full of ideas. But why? Was there something more he might know, some piece of information he might have been given? *Like something that might be in a spy dossier,* Marcos thought.

"Clues are usually written in words, right?" JJ continued.

"Of course they are," said Basil. "What else would they be written in?"

"Well, the clue Anya figured out was kind of written in numbers," JJ said. "In classical music the notes are the words. So maybe the clue is really *in* the music. Not the book, but in one of the pieces."

"That's an interesting idea," Marcos said. "But how do we know which piece? And how do we know what it says?"

"That's kind of where I got stuck, too," said JJ.

"So we're right back where we started," said Anya, sighing heavily from her chair.

"Don't give up," Marcos said. "I have a feeling that JJ is right about this. Let's just keep thinking. Titus, did your grandfather have a favorite piece by Grieg? Anything you can remember him playing a lot?"

"Did my grandfather have a favorite piece by Grieg?" he repeated. His expression went blank for a moment, again as if he was waiting for the answer to come to him. Then he said, "Yes, he did. It's called 'In the Hall of the Mountain King.'"

"Is that in the book?" Marcos asked Kat.

"Yes," Kat said, turning to a page in the book. "It's right here. And there's something written here. It's hard to make out." She squinted at the page, then said, "This is odd. It says 'Don't forget to use the metronome.' Only the ending is spelled G-N-O-M-E."

JJ laughed, causing the others to turn and look at him.

"Why is that funny?" Basil asked.

"'In the Hall of the Mountain King' is about an underground cavern filled with gold and jewels," he said. "The Mountain King sits on a throne while goblins and gnomes dance around him. Get it, a metro*gnome*? It's a pun."

"Oh yes," Basil said. "I see. That's very clever wordplay."

"What's a metro-thingy?" asked one of the Popps.

"It's a thing you use to help you keep time when you're practicing the piano," JJ explained.

"You really know a lot about this," Marcos said, wondering once more whether there was more to the pop singer than people knew. *Like maybe he's a spy*, Marcos thought. It was seeming more and more likely.

JJ sighed. "Okay," he said. "I'll tell you. But you can't tell anybody else. I have an image and all that."

He waited for them all to nod their agreement not to tell, then continued. "My real name isn't JJ Jay," he said. "It's Andrew Blevowitz. And before I became a singer I kind of played classical piano."

"Kind of?" Titus said.

"Well, more than kind of," JJ admitted. "I was actually really good. I mean, *really* good, like I played all over the world good. I even made a couple of records. But I really wanted to be a singer, so I made up JJ Jay. And the rest is history."

"Wow," said Marcos. "I didn't see that coming."

"Yeah, well, that info doesn't leave this room," JJ said. "If it does, I'll know where it came from. Now, give me that music."

Kat handed him the book, and JJ went and sat at the grand piano. He lifted the keyboard cover and ran his fingers over the keys. The notes filled the room with a beautiful sound.

"This is a nice piano," JJ said. Then he looked at the music, which he'd set on the stand in front of him. "Here goes nothing."

"What are we listening for?" Anya asked.

"Your guess is as good as mine," said JJ. "I'm just playing."

He started playing, and Marcos was amazed at how good he was. His fingers flew over the keys as if they knew where to go without him doing anything. The music poured out of the piano.

"Is this his new single?" asked a Popp sister, and they all shushed her.

Marcos really had no idea what he was listening for, but he was enjoying JJ's playing. He closed his eyes and tried to imagine what it might look like in the Mountain King's hall, and he had no trouble picturing the gnomes and goblins dancing around, holding jewels in their hands and tossing gold into the air.

All of the sudden, JJ stopped playing. Marcos opened his eyes.

"What's wrong?" Titus asked.

JJ pointed to the wall. "Look for yourself," he said.

They all turned. Earlier, a life-sized portrait of a man dressed in old-fashioned clothes and with a black-and-white dog sitting beside him had hung there.

But now the painting was gone, and they were looking into an open doorway.

CHAPTER SEVEN

Marcos peered into the opening in the wall. A set of stairs descended into darkness below.

"Where do these go?" he asked Titus.

"I have no idea," Titus said. "I've never seen these before."

"Well, there's one way to find out," Kat said.

The Popp sisters shook their heads. "We are *not* going down there," they said in unison.

"Fine," Kat said. "You can stay here and wait for us."

"By ourselves?" one said.

"We'll come," said the second twin.

Kat went first. She was followed by Titus,

then Basil, Anya, the Popp twins, JJ, and finally Marcos. Ordinarily he wouldn't have taken a place at the end of the line, but he wanted to be able to keep an eye on everyone. He thought it was better to be in the back so that nobody could escape back up the stairs.

This turned out not to be a problem, for when Marcos was six steps down the stairs, the picture that had been covering the doorway slid back into place, shutting them in. Fortunately, small lights in the ceiling came on, but they were dim and it was still difficult to see anything clearly. Marcos turned around and ran back to the door. But there was no handle there, no button, no secret lever that would open it back up. There was just a solid piece of wood. He banged on it several times to make sure, but nothing happened.

"Great," said one of the Popp girls. "Good going."

"I didn't do anything," said Marcos. "The door must be rigged to shut after a certain amount of time."

"Well, now we *have* to go down," said JJ. "Might as well get going."

The stairs seemed to go on forever, taking them farther and farther down. After a while the Popps started complaining about their feet hurting, and Marcos tuned out their voices by trying once more to identify the ROGUE agent in their midst. Was it Kat? JJ? Maybe Basil or Anya? Everybody was a suspect at this point, except possibly the Popp twins. They just weren't smart enough to be spies. *Which of course means they probably* are *spies,* he told himself, remembering what Principal Booker had once said about not letting appearances deceive.

Finally the stairs ended, emptying out into a stone-walled tunnel wide enough for two of them to walk side by side. This time Marcos found himself in front with Titus, while the still-whining Popp sisters followed, with Anya and JJ behind them and Basil and Kat bringing up the rear.

"How far down do you think we are?" Titus asked as they walked.

"Quite a way," said Marcos. "I tried counting the steps, and if I'm right, we're about three hundred feet below the first floor of the house."

"Underground?" said Titus. "No wonder it's so cold."

The tunnel was indeed chilly. Also, the stone walls were wet with moisture. Despite everything, though, Marcos was excited. This was a real adventure, and he felt like an explorer discovering an ancient pyramid or lost city.

Then they turned a corner and Titus let out a scream that echoed through the tunnel. This made the Popp sisters scream, too, and for a moment even Marcos was frozen in place as he looked up at the monster standing in front of them.

At least nine feet tall, it had the muscular body of a man but the head of a bull. Its eyes glowed red, and steam came from its nostrils in little bursts. Light glinted off enormous horns that almost touched the sides of the tunnel. Marcos waited for it to attack, but it remained still.

"It's a Minotaur," Basil said, pushing past the still-screaming Popp twins and coming closer. "A statue of a Minotaur."

"A statue," Titus said. "Of course it's a statue. There's no such thing as a Minotaur." He laughed loudly, which Marcos knew was to hide his embarrassment over being scared by a statue.

"What's a Minotaur?" Anya asked. "It looks

like a bull man."

"That's exactly what it is," said Basil. "In Greek mythology, the Minotaur was a monster who lived inside a labyrinth."

"A what?" asked one of the twins.

"A labyrinth," Basil replied. "A maze. He killed anyone who became trapped inside. Anyway, the Minotaur was eventually defeated by Theseus."

"The question is, what is he doing here?" JJ said.

Marcos looked past the Minotaur. "Wait here a minute," he said.

He slipped behind the statue and walked into another tunnel. This one went on for about twenty feet before stopping. There were tunnels continuing on to both the left and the right. Marcos returned to the group.

"Just like I thought," he said. "We're about to enter a labyrinth."

"Great," said Anya. "And how do we get through it without a map?"

"We could split up and go in both directions," Titus suggested.

"Yeah, because that always ends really well,"

said Kat. "I say we pick one direction and go that way, marking the places where we turn in case we need to go back and try again."

"There's an easier way," Marcos said. "I read once that if you walk through a maze always keeping one hand—always the same hand—on the wall, you won't get lost. If you come to a dead end, you just turn around and keep your opposite hand on the wall. That takes you back to where you started; then you know the right path is the other way."

"There's just one problem," Kat said. "That only works on one kind of maze: a really simple one. If this isn't that kind, we'll still end up lost."

"How about this?" said Marcos. "We'll try my way first. If it doesn't work, we'll come back here and try your way."

Kat thought for a minute. "All right," she said grudgingly. "But I bet it won't work."

Ignoring her, Marcos led the way into the maze. He kept his right hand on the wall, and every time they came to a place where the tunnel split off, he made the turn that allowed him to keep his hand on the wall without switching sides. After a while he lost track of how many turns they made, and he wondered whether maybe Kat was right. He was just about to suggest they turn back when the tunnel made one final twist and opened up into a cavernous space.

Marcos couldn't believe what he was looking at. They were standing at the bottom of a set of wide stone steps that led up to what appeared to be an ancient stone temple. There were columns all around it, and a dome, and statues of strange creatures everywhere. Everything was lit by pale light that came from an unseen source, making it look as though the temple and everything around it were under water.

"Awesome!" JJ said as he emerged into the cavern.

"This has got to be the treasure," said Kat, for once sounding impressed.

"Does this means we win?" asked one of the Popp girls.

"And what do we win?" asked the other.

Titus, who had dashed up the steps ahead of them, called, "Come on! You guys have got to see this!"

The others joined him outside the entrance to the temple. Inside, directly under the dome, was a huge statue. Even larger than the one of the Minotaur, this one was of a merman. He appeared to be rising from the waves. His thick beard was filled with starfish and seaweed and tiny crabs, and fish leaped out of the water all around him. In his hand he held a huge shell, which was raised to his lips.

"Who is he?" Marcos asked.

Beside him, Titus was staring at the statue with wide eyes. "The Spirit of the Sea," he said. "He found him. He really found him."

"Who found him?" asked Basil.

"My grandfather," Titus said. "He would never say if he really had or not."

"Why wouldn't he want anyone to know?" Anya said.

Titus moved closer to the statue. "Because of where it came from," he said.

"Which is where?" Kat asked impatiently.

Titus turned and looked at her, a big grin on his face. "Atlantis," he said. "The lost city of Atlantis."

CHAPTER EIGHT

Atlantis?" Kat said. "Atlantis isn't real. It's just a story."

Titus shook his head. "It existed," he said. "And my grandfather found it."

"Then why didn't he tell anyone?" asked Kat. "Wouldn't he want everyone to know he'd discovered it?"

"Not yet," Titus answered. He was walking around the statue of the Spirit of the Sea, running his hand over the stone waves.

"What do you mean, 'not yet'?" Marcos asked him.

"What?" said Titus. "Oh, I mean he was waiting until he, um, had everything cataloged and preserved. He didn't want anyone else finding the city and ruining it or whatever."

Something was odd about the way Titus was speaking. He didn't sound like himself.

Marcos couldn't believe they were looking at a statue from the legendary city of Atlantis. But why were the temple and its statue hidden so far underground? And how had the clues led them there if nobody knew about it? Something wasn't adding up.

"When do we get our prize?"

One of the Popp twins was standing beside Marcos, looking at the statue. She seemed bored.

"I don't know," Marcos told her. "I guess when we go back to the mansion."

"And how are we going to do *that*?" she asked.

Marcos thought for a moment. "Actually, I don't know," he admitted. "Maybe Titus does."

The girl rolled her eyes. "That's another thing," she said. "I think there's something wrong with him."

Marcos looked at her. "Why do you say that?"

"Well," she said, sounding excited, as if she were sharing a juicy piece of gossip. "Fanta reminded me that we've met him before. In Switzerland? Our family was there on a ski vacation?"

Everything she said sounded like a question. She seemed to expect an answer, so Marcos said, "Right. I love Switzerland," Shasta continued. "They have awesome cheese and stuff. Anyway, Titus was there, too. I remember he was wearing a really cute sweater. Well, Fanta remembered, and then so did I."

Because you share a brain, Marcos thought unkindly. He immediately felt bad for thinking such a thing. Still, Shasta really wasn't the smartest person he'd ever met.

"Well, a while ago Fanta said something to Titus about how great Switzerland was. Then he said, 'I wouldn't know. I've never been there.' That's kind of weird. Who wouldn't remember going to Switzerland? And anyway, how could he forget meeting us?"

That part, Marcos thought, was true. The Popp

twins were certainly unforgettable, even if it was for all the wrong reasons.

"I don't know," he said to the girl. "Maybe he didn't understand what Fanta said."

"Please," said Shasta. "It's not like she used a bunch of big words. You know, like that Kat girl does. What's with her anyway? She's kind of stuck-up."

Marcos didn't reply. He was looking at Titus. While the others walked around the temple, Titus was inside it. Fanta was standing just outside, and he was motioning to her to come in.

The girl hesitated, then walked inside. At that moment, Titus jumped up onto the statue. His hand went into his pocket, and when it came out again it was holding something blue. He pushed this into one of the statue's eyes. Then he leaped from the statue and darted outside the temple, leaving Fanta inside.

The statue's eye glowed. A moment later there was a brilliant flash of blue light. Someone screamed, and then the light went out. But the statue's eye still glowed.

"What was that?" Kat said, looking at Titus.

They were all looking at Titus, who was clapping his hands together and laughing loudly. "It worked!" he shouted. "It really worked!"

"Where's Fanta?" Shasta asked, looking around. "She was just here."

Titus turned to her. "Don't worry," he said. "She's somewhere safe. Well, maybe. I'm not exactly sure where she went."

"What do you mean, you don't know where she went?" said Marcos.

"I suppose there's no harm in telling you now," Titus said. Something about his voice seemed different, less careful and more haughty, and even his posture had changed.

"The Blue Carbuncle is more than just a stone," he began. "It's a key."

"A key to what?" JJ asked.

"To this," said Titus, indicating the statue. "You see, it's not just a statue. It's a machine. The most important machine the world has ever seen."

"A machine?" said Kat. "What does it do?"

Titus grinned unpleasantly. "It's a transporter," he said. "A teleporter, actually. My grandfather created it using technology he discovered in Atlantis. Well, he re-created it."

"What's a teleporter?" Shasta asked. "And where's Fanta?"

"It moves things from one place to another," Marcos explained to her. "Only it does it by turning the thing—or person—into millions of tiny particles. Then it brings those particles back together somewhere else."

Shasta looked confused, but Marcos didn't know how else to explain it to her.

"A crude explanation," Titus said. "But basically accurate. You see, this isn't just a temple. It's a chamber. Whatever is in here when the Carbuncle is activated is teleported somewhere else. The Carbuncle is the key that focuses the energy."

"How do you tell it where to go?" said Basil.

"Well, now, that's the one problem," Titus said. "We don't really know. I mean, there's a set of controls over here," he continued, pointing to what looked like a large seashell. "But we'll have to do some more tests before we know exactly how to use them."

"You mean, you don't know where Fanta is?" Marcos inquired.

"I kind of know where she is," said Titus. "As long as the diaries are right, that is."

"Diaries?" JJ said. "What diaries?"

"Napoleon Coin's diaries," Titus answered.

This was the first time Marcos had heard Titus refer to Napoleon as anything but "Grandfather." He wondered why this time he had used his name. Then a number of things fell into place, like the tumblers of a lock moving into position, allowing the lock to open.

"Who are you?" he asked Titus. "Because I don't think you're Titus Coin."

Everyone else looked at him as if he must be crazy. Everyone except Titus, who cocked his head.

"I was going to ask you the same question," he said. "I know who all of them are, but I've never heard of you."

"I'm Marcos Elias," Marcos said, falling back on his cover story. "I design video games."

"I don't think so," Titus said. "You see, while we've been figuring out the clues Napoleon Coin left behind, my associates have been trying to find information on you. And do you know what? There isn't any. Nothing. Why is that?"

"Maybe they aren't looking hard enough," said Marcos. He had a feeling the game they'd been playing had suddenly turned dangerous. He also had a feeling he knew who Titus's associates were.

"What's going on here?" Anya asked.

Titus, still keeping an eye on Marcos, said, "What's going on is that you've all helped me solve Napoleon Coin's greatest mystery."

Suddenly, Marcos understood. "You're all on the same team for a reason," he said to Anya. "You each have special skills that would be helpful in solving a series of mysteries."

Titus nodded. "That's exactly right," he said. "We weren't sure exactly what skills would be needed, so we selected people with a range of talents. And you've each contributed something vitally important to my mission. Well, most of you have," he added, looking meaningfully at Shasta.

"You still haven't told us who you are," Marcos reminded him. "Who you *really* are."

Titus hesitated, then said, "I don't suppose it will hurt to tell you. My name is Gerard Budge."

CHAPTER NINE

Budge?" Marcos said. "As in Chrysanthemum Budge, Napoleon Coin's personal assistant?"

"Yes," said Gerard. "Chrysanthemum Budge is my mother."

"I still don't understand," said Anya.

"And if you're not the real Titus, where is he?" JJ added.

"So many questions," said Gerard. "First of all, the real Titus is somewhere safe. He hasn't been harmed, if that's what you're worried about. As for why, that's a long story. You see, my mother served Napoleon Coin faithfully for more than thirty years. He shared all of his secrets with her, and she kept them. But when he died, he left her nothing. Not one cent. Not even an antique carpet or a necklace or a horse. Nothing. He left everything to Titus."

"She must have done something to deserve it," Shasta suggested.

"She did not!" Gerard screamed. "She did everything for him, and he betrayed her."

He cleared his throat and smoothed his hair, calming himself.

"The only thing my mother was left with was a clue," he continued. "She found it in a notebook when she was cleaning out Napoleon's desk. What she discovered was that the Blue Carbuncle was a key to an invention—Napoleon Coin's greatest invention. The only problem was, it didn't say what the invention was or where to find it. She had some ideas, of course, based on the things Napoleon was interested in. And one of them was that the machine might be used for teleportation. Of course, she also thought it might be a machine that turned lead into gold."

"That would certainly be handy," said Basil. "Why, you could make everyone in the world wealthy, and—"

"Shut up," Gerard ordered. "I'm not finished."

"This really is a long story," JJ remarked. "Can we have the short version?"

Gerard sighed. "Whatever," he said, as if they were ruining his big moment. "In addition to the information about the Carbuncle, she found the first clue that we were given tonight."

"The one about the book?" said Anya.

"Yes," Gerard confirmed. "It was scribbled on a napkin tucked into the notebook. And then you all helped find and decipher the remaining clues, which led us here."

"So Napoleon Coin hid all of those clues?" said JJ. "How come, if he didn't want anyone to find this place?"

"He did want someone to find it," Marcos said, having thought about this very question for some time. "Someone who would use the invention for good. I'm guessing he put the clues in place hoping that someday someone smart enough to figure them out would come along and follow the path here."

"Oh, very good," said Gerard, clapping his hands together slowly. "Did you figure that out all by yourself?"

"You really are a little snot," Kat said to Gerard.

"And you're an obnoxious know-it-all," Gerard countered. "I guess that makes us even."

"So you kidnapped Titus and you took his place," said Marcos. "Very clever."

"Fortunately, I look enough like him that it wasn't too hard," Gerard said. "Some hair dye, different clothes, a fake nose, and ta-da—I'm Napoleon Coin's grandson. And of course my mother knew all the details of Titus's life because she'd been around since the day he was born. All she had to do was feed me the information when I needed it."

"Can we just figure out where my sister is?" Shasta interrupted.

"Possibly," said Gerard. "Let me just confer with my associates."

He fiddled with something in his ear, frowned,

and fiddled some more. "Mom?" he said. "Mom, are you there?"

"Now he wants his mommy," JJ joked.

"Mom?" Gerard said, sounding slightly panicked. "Mom!"

He pulled something from his ear and threw it to the floor. "Stupid comm unit," he shouted. "What a piece of junk."

So that's how he always knew things when he needed to, Marcos thought. *And I bet that's why* my *earpiece stopped working. His signal was blocking it.*

Confirming his suspicion to be true, Marcos's earpiece returned to life. "Marcos?" said Tinker's voice. "Are you there? We managed to unblock the signal."

"I'm here," Marcos said.

"Where are you?" asked Tinker.

"I'm in a temple from Atlantis," Marcos answered.

"Very funny," said Tinker.

"I'm serious," Marcos told her.

"Who are you talking to?" Gerard yelled.

"Your mother," said Marcos, teasing him.

"What's going on there?" Tinker asked.

"Too much to tell you right now," said Marcos. "What you need to worry about is finding Titus Coin. The real Titus Coin. The one with me is an imposter. He's working for ROGUE."

Gerard hissed. "Only a SPY Academy student would know that!"

Out of the corner of his eye, Marcos noticed that Kat had slowly made her way over to the shell housing the controls for the teleportation device. She looked at him, cut her eyes to Gerard, and tilted her head.

She wants me to get Gerard into the machine, Marcos thought.

Tinker was still talking in his ear as Marcos made a decision. Rushing up the steps, he hit Gerard in the middle of his chest and pushed as hard as he could. Gerard flew backward, right between two of the pillars, and hit the merman's tail. He opened his mouth in a loud scream of pain, and right at that moment the blue light flashed again and he disappeared.

"Now where did *he* go?" Shasta wailed.

"Do you know?" Marcos asked Kat.

"Maybe," she said. "There's some kind of writing here, but it's nothing I've ever seen. But I think these are numbers on the dials. If I'm right, I sent him 450 feet up and 730 feet to the left. I'm fairly certain—well, kind of certain—that that puts him somewhere in the west wing of the mansion. Probably in an attic or something."

"If you're right," Basil said.

"I suppose I could be wrong," Kat admitted. "This writing is really weird."

"Then where would he be?" Anya asked.

Kat shrugged. "Just about anywhere. Alaska, maybe, or in the middle of the Yellow Sea. Possibly Mars."

"Now, *that* would be cool," JJ commented.

"Do you mean my sister could be on another *planet*?" Shasta said.

"Probably not," said Kat. "I'm pretty sure I know what these numbers mean. Maybe."

Shasta sat down on the steps and started to cry. Everyone looked at one another, and finally Anya went over and sat beside her. Putting her arm around Shasta, she said, "I'm sure Fanta is all right."

"But she could be on Mars!" Shasta wailed. "Or Alaska!"

"Alaska isn't so bad," JJ remarked.

Shasta continued to cry, while Marcos thought about what to do next. Then he remembered that his connection to Tinker was back on.

"Tinker?" he said. "Is there any way for you to get a trace on my earpiece?"

"Let me try," said Tinker. "No. You're too far away."

"The rock is probably blocking it," Marcos said. "All right. Like I said, you guys try to find Titus. I'm going to go after Gerard."

"Don't do anything stupid," Tinker said.

Marcos took a deep breath. "I'll try," he said.

He walked up to the temple and stood beside the statue.

"Kat, send me where you sent Gerard."

"But we don't really know where that is," Basil reminded him.

"It could be Alaska!" Shasta sobbed.

"Just do it," Marcos said to Kat. "Oh, but first take this."

He removed his earpiece and tossed it to JJ. "That will keep you in contact with the rest of my team. They'll help you find your way out of here."

"But how will they find you?" JJ asked.

"I'll figure that out later," said Marcos. He looked at Kat. "Now do whatever it is you do to make this thing work."

As Kat reached for the controls, Marcos shut his eyes. If he was going to be scattered into a million pieces, he didn't want to see it.

A bright flash lit up the temple. This was followed by a whooshing sound, and Marcos felt his body tingle all over, as if he'd touched a live electrical wire. It didn't hurt, but it felt strange. He also felt as if he were moving through the air at an incredible speed.

Then it was over. His body stopped tingling, and the light faded away. He felt something solid under his feet, and the air around him was warm. For a moment he thought he'd been blinded, as he couldn't see anything, but then he realized that he was simply standing in the dark.

After a time, his eyes adjusted to the low light and he looked around. There was no sign of Gerard. But moonlight shone through a window at one end of the room, illuminating piles of boxes, some items draped with sheets, and some other things that were hidden by the shadows. The smell of dust filled Marcos's nose, and he sneezed.

I'm in an attic, he realized. *Kat was right.*

He assumed the attic was part of the Coin mansion. Not that it really mattered. What mattered was finding Gerard.

And he was nowhere to be seen.

CHAPTER TEN

Gerard!" Marcos called out. "I know you're here. You might as well come out. The game's over, and you lost."

There was no reply, but somewhere in the darkness Marcos heard a sound like someone trying to sneak his way through stacks of boxes.

He stood still, listening, and the sound stopped.

"You can't hide forever," Marcos said.

A figure flew at him out of the darkness. Marcos dodged it and stuck his foot out, trying to trip Gerard. Instead he felt something hard run over his toes. He yelped.

The figure clattered to the floor. At first it

appeared to be the body of a woman without a head, arms, or legs. Then Marcos realized that it was a dummy, the kind dressmakers use to hang pieces of material on while sewing clothes.

But then something else came out of the darkness, and this something was yelling at the top of his lungs. Marcos had no time to turn away before Gerard was on top of him, beating at him with his fists.

"You're not going to win!" Gerard yelled in Marcos's ear. "My mother deserves a reward, and she's going to get it!"

They fell to the floor, with Gerard on top. The air was knocked out of Marcos as his back struck the rough wood boards. For what seemed like forever, he couldn't move. Then he was able to breathe again.

He grabbed Gerard's hair (he wasn't proud of this, and left this part out when he told the story later) and pulled as hard as he could. Gerard yelled, and for a moment he stopped hitting Marcos. This was all the opportunity he needed. Rolling sideways, he pushed Gerard off of him and scrambled to his feet.

Gerard, holding one hand to his head, jumped up as well. He was breathing hard, and he glared at Marcos with pure hatred. Then he looked around and grabbed a doll that was lying on top of a dresser. He hurled it at Marcos, and followed it with a teddy bear he found on the floor.

"You might want to try something that isn't so soft," Marcos taunted him.

Gerard kept picking up objects and throwing them at Marcos as he slowly made his way backward through the attic. Marcos, busy dodging the missiles, tried to follow him, but couldn't do it quickly enough. Gerard was getting away.

When Gerard thought that he had a clear shot to the door, he turned and ran. Marcos knew he had only one chance to stop him. Looking around, he spied a croquet ball that had slipped out of its holder and come to rest next to a stack of hatboxes.

Marcos picked the ball up and rolled it toward Gerard. The ball bounced over the floorboards and went between Gerard's feet, tripping him. He let out a yelp, flailed his arms as he tried unsuccessfully to maintain his balance, and fell to the floor.

Marcos ran to him and knelt down, putting one

knee on his back so that Gerard groaned. Looking around, he found an old bathrobe lying on the floor and pulled the belt from it. He used this to tie Gerard's wrists together behind his back.

"That should hold you," he said.

Gerard said some very unpleasant things, but Marcos ignored him. He was trying to figure out how he was going to get Gerard out of the attic and back to wherever the rest of the team was. But since he'd given his communicator to the kids still underground in the temple, he had no way of contacting anyone.

Just then he heard somebody pounding on the door. Then he heard his name.

"Marcos!" someone shouted.

It was Jen.

"In here!" Marcos called back.

A moment later the door opened and Jen stepped inside. Zeke was with her.

"How'd you find me?" Marcos asked them.

"Kat remembered the coordinates," Jen said.

"So, you found them," Marcos said, relieved to know everyone was okay.

Zeke nodded. "Tinker was able to trace the

signal from your earpiece," he said. "She thinks the depth of the temple was blocking it. She got through for just a few seconds, but it was enough to get us a location. Man, that place is awesome."

"We can talk about how awesome it is later, boys," Jen said. "Right now we have to get this one downstairs."

Marcos hauled Gerard to his feet. The boy said nothing as they led him out of the attic and down some stairs to the next floor. Three sets of stairs later, they were in the hallway that led to the library. They went there, where they found Shasta, JJ, Kat, Anya, and Basil waiting. Tinker and Narhari were there with them.

"Look what we found," Jen said as they brought Gerard in.

"Nice catch," said Tinker. "And you'll be happy to hear that we found the real Titus, too. He was tied up in a shed in the garden."

"Oh yeah?" said Zeke. "How'd you do that?"

"Easy," Tinker said. "I told Chrysanthemum Budge that we'd send her kid to Antarctica if she didn't cooperate." She looked at Gerard. "She crumbled like a stale cookie," she told him.

"Where is she?" Gerard said, sounding like a frightened boy and not a superspy.

"Down in the kitchen," Narhari said. "With the guards from the front gate. They'll hand her over to the police once we're out of here."

"Police?" Gerard yelped, his eyes widening.

Narhari ignored him. "They also rounded up all the party guests and told them they had to leave because of a gas leak. That cleared the place out in a hurry."

"There's something I've been wondering about," Basil said. "We all saw the Blue Carbuncle in its case. But Gerard had it in his pocket. How did he do that?"

"Oh, that's easy," Shasta said. "The one in the case is a fake."

They all turned and looked at her in surprise.

"How did you know that?" Kat asked.

Shasta gave her a look. "Please, I know a fake catbuckle when I see one."

"Carbuncle," JJ said. "It's a carbuncle."

"Whatever," said Shasta. "Anyway, I could tell it was a fake. Do you think Fanta and I wear our real jewels when we go to parties? You always have a set of fakes. That way, you don't have to worry about people stealing them."

"But if you always wear the fakes, what's the point of having the real ones?" JJ asked her.

"Can we talk about something else?" said Shasta. "Like, where's my sister?"

"Oh, about that," Tinker said. "We found her."

Shasta looked afraid. "She's not in Alaska, is she?" she asked. "She really hates the jungle. It makes her hair frizzy."

"There's no jungle in—" Tinker began, but Marcos motioned for her to stop. He knew Shasta didn't care where Alaska was or what it was like. She just wanted to know where her sister was.

"She's in Disneyland," Tinker said. "In California," she added. "In America."

"I know where Disneyland is," said Shasta, sounding offended. "It's where Cinderella lives. Is she okay?"

Tinker nodded. "She's fine," she said. "She was

transported into the Pirates of the Caribbean ride. Popped up in someone's boat and scared them silly."

"So, Gerard and Chrysanthemum have been caught, Titus has been found, and Fanta has been located," Marcos said. "I think that's everything, right?"

"Just about," said a voice from the doorway.

Principal Booker walked into the library. He stood in front of Gerard and looked at him for a long time. "You're in a great deal of trouble, young man," he said.

"Am I going to go to jail?" Gerard asked. He sounded as though he might start crying.

"No," Principal Booker said. "Not if you cooperate and tell the police everything. But tell me this: How did your mother get mixed up with my brother, Maximus?"

"He told her he would give her half of everything he made from the invention," Gerard said.

Cornelius nodded. "I see," he said. "Greed always seems to lead to trouble." He patted Gerard on the shoulder. "It's time for you to go downstairs now," he said. "But once this matter is cleared up, I want your mother to bring you to me. We might be able to make a *good* spy out of you yet."

"Really?" said Gerard, sounding hopeful.

"I said *might*," Principal Booker reminded him. "Now, go with Narhari. And don't try anything funny. She's a black belt in three different martial arts."

"Are you really?" Gerard asked as she took him by the arm and led him out of the library.

"You don't want to find out," said Narhari.

"Well," Principal Booker said to the rest of the team. "How did you enjoy your midterm?"

Marcos looked at Tinker, Zeke, and Jen. No one seemed to want to speak first. Then, all at once, all four said, "We loved it!"

Principal Booker smiled. "You did very well," he said.

"So we all get A's?" Marcos asked.

Their teacher smiled slyly. "On this test, yes," he said. "But wait until you see what I have in store for your final."